SHERLOCK HOLMES

SHERLOCK HOLMES
Selected Stories

By Sir Arthur Conan Doyle

Adapted by Diana Stewart
Illustrated by Don Toht

Raintree Publishers • Milwaukee • Toronto • Melbourne • London

Library of Congress Number: 79-24106

2 3 4 5 6 7 8 9 0 84 83 82 81

Printed in the United States of America.

Library of Congress Cataloging in Publication Data

Stewart, Diana.
Sherlock Holmes.

CONTENTS: A scandal in Bohemia. — The adventure
of the speckled band. — Silver Blaze. — The man with
the twisted lip. — The Red-headed League.
1. Detective and mystery stories, English.
[1. Mystery and detective stories. 2. Short
stories] I. Doyle, Arthur Conan, Sir. 1859-1930.
Selection. II. Toht, Don. III. Title.
PZ7.S84878Sh   [Fic]   79-24106
ISBN 0-8172-1657-X lib. bdg.

CONTENTS

A SCANDAL IN BOHEMIA

1

I had not seen much of Sherlock Holmes since my marriage. One night, however, as I was returning home from visiting a patient, I passed by his house on Baker Street and decided to stop in.

"Watson, my dear fellow," he greeted me, "I can see that marriage suits you very well. But I did not know you had returned to practicing medicine."

"How do you know now that I have, Holmes?" I asked.

"My dear friend," he laughed, "when a man comes through the door smelling of medicine and there is a lump in his top hat where he has put his stethoscope, what else am I to think?"

"Holmes," I remarked, "you continually amaze me!"

"I also see," he continued, "that you have been out walking in the rain recently and that you have a very careless servant girl."

"My dear Holmes, you are right again, but how could you know?"

"Your boots, Watson. Around the sole are signs of mud that the careless servant has not entirely removed."

"How do you do it?" I asked, puzzled. "I see the same things you do, but I do not come up with the same conclusions."

"Ah, Watson, that is the point. You *see*, but you do not *notice*. For example, you have often come up my stairs. How many steps are there?"

"How many? I have no idea."

"There are seventeen. Do you understand? I both *see* and *notice*. That is the difference."

He smiled and sat in a large chair with his long legs stretched out in front of him.

"Sit down, my friend," he invited. "I am about to have a very interesting visitor, and if you would like, you may stay and hear about my next case."

A few moments later a man was shown into the room. He was very richly dressed and wore a mask over his eyes. He looked nervously at me before turning to Holmes.

"You are Sherlock Holmes?" he asked in a deep voice with a strong German accent.

"Yes, your Majesty, I am," Holmes answered.

The man was startled and with a cry tore the mask from his face.

"But how did you know who I was?"

"As soon as you spoke, I recognized you as the King of Bohemia. Would you care to tell me why you are here and what I can do for you?"

"I am in a very bad situation, Holmes," the king replied. "I have come to you because of your reputation of being able to solve the most difficult of cases. I am being blackmailed by a woman here in London who used to be a . . . a very close friend. Her name is Irene Adler. She thought I would marry her, but she is a singer, and I must marry someone of royal blood."

"And how is she blackmailing you?"

"I am to be married soon to the daughter of the King of Scandinavia. This singer threatens that if I announce the engagement, she will give the newspaper a picture of the two of us together. It would create a scandal, and my marriage would be called off. I must have the picture back!"

"Have you offered to buy it back?"

"Yes, but she will not take money. I have even had people break into her home to steal it, but they could find nothing."

"How long do I have?" Holmes asked.

"You have only three days. My engagement will be announced on Monday," the King replied.

"Return to your hotel and wait for me to send you word. Watson, meet me here tomorrow at three o'clock."

When I arrived the next day, Holmes had not returned. As I sat down, the door opened and in came an old drunken workman. I had often seen Holmes in disguise, but I was not sure this was he. I watched with interest as he removed the old, torn coat, the gray wig, and the make-up on his face. It was indeed Holmes.

"I have had a most interesting day, Watson," he remarked and rubbed his hands together in satisfaction. "I followed Miss Adler to the Church of St. Monica. There she met a man, a lawyer named Godfrey Norton. I waited outside the door. A moment later Norton came out, grabbed me by the arm, and dragged me inside. Watson, I became the witness to the marriage of Godfrey Norton and Irene Adler!"

"But what about the picture, Holmes? Did you find it?"

"No, but I am sure that it is still in her house."

"How could it be?" I asked. "The king has already had the house searched."

"But he did not know where to look. I have a plan that will show us where the picture is hidden. Will you help me?"

I was not pleased with what Holmes had in mind for me, but I agreed. I was even less pleased when I first saw Irene Adler. She was a beautiful woman, and very charming. I stood by her house as she stepped alone from her carriage later that afternoon. She was immediately surrounded by a group of beggars and rough-looking men that Holmes had hired. When a fight broke out, Holmes arrived disguised as an old priest. He sent the men on their way and pretended to fall and injure himself. Carefully the lady's servants helped him into the house to recover.

Now it was time for my part of the plot. Into the open window I threw a smoke bomb and began to cry, "Fire!" Thick smoke curled out the window and I saw figures

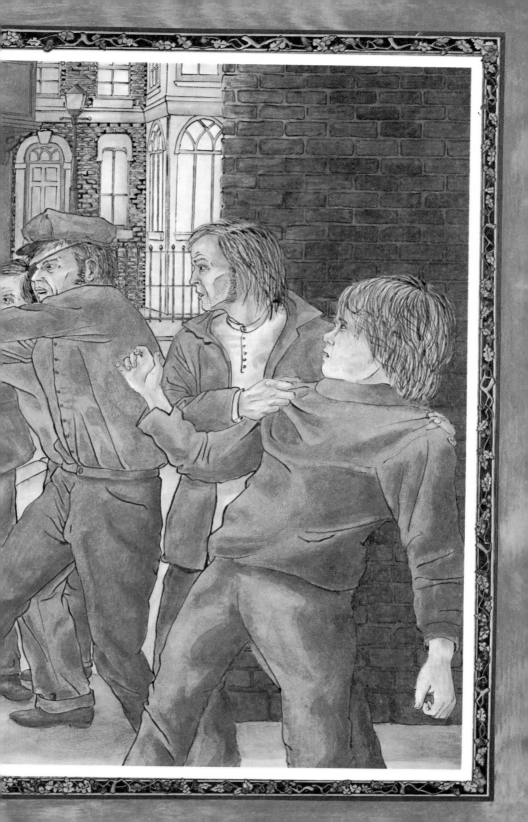

inside rushing about. Then I heard Holmes assuring them that it was a false alarm. It was all over in a few minutes. I hurried down the street to the place I was to meet Holmes. He soon arrived looking very pleased with himself.

"Did you get the picture?" I asked.

"No, there were too many servants around, but I now know exactly where it is. We will return tomorrow and get it."

"But how, Holmes?" I inquired.

"Very simple, my dear Watson," Holmes replied. "When a person believes there is a fire in his house, he will try to rescue his most valuable things. When you cried fire, Irene Adler rushed to a secret panel in the wall. By then I pretended to recover and told her there was no danger. Quickly she closed the panel. Tomorrow we will go back, open the secret panel, and take the picture."

The next day Holmes called the King and asked him to go with us to Irene Adler's house. When we arrived, we were surprised to find the lady had gone! Holmes opened the panel, but instead of finding the picture, inside was a letter addressed to him. It read:

Dear Mr. Sherlock Holmes,

You really did it very well. You took me in completely. Until after the alarm of fire, I had not a suspicion. But when I found how I had betrayed myself, I began to think. I had been warned against you months ago. And yet I found it hard to think badly of such a dear, kind old clergyman. But, you know, I have been trained as an actress myself. Male costume is nothing new to me.

So I have taken the picture and have left for France with my husband. Tell the King that I am now happily married, and he has nothing more to fear from me. He did me a great wrong, and I am keeping the picture to make sure that he never bothers me again in the future.

Very truly yours,
Irene Adler Norton

"What a woman!" the King cried. "It is too bad that she was a commoner. She would have made a wonderful queen!"

And that was how a great scandal that threatened the King of Bohemia was brought to a happy end. That was also how the best of plans of Mr. Sherlock Holmes were beaten by a woman's wit. He used to laugh at women and think them inferior to men. No more.

THE ADVENTURE
OF THE SPECKLED BAND
2

I have notes on over seventy cases from Sherlock
Holmes' files. Some are comic and some are tragic—all of
them are unusual. One of the strangest happened before I
was married and still lived with Holmes on Baker Street.

Holmes woke me very early one morning and asked me
to meet a new client who had called. Quickly I dressed and
joined them in the library. I have never seen a young
woman so terrified! Her face was drawn and grey and her
eyes looked like those of a hunted animal.

"This is Helen Stoner, Watson," Holmes said. "She has
come to us for help. First, Miss Stoner, you must tell Dr.
Watson and me what is frightening you."

"That is the trouble, Mr. Holmes. I am not sure!"

"Then I suggest you begin at the beginning and tell us
about yourself," Holmes said gently.

"I live in Surrey with my stepfather—Dr. Roylott. He
was once a doctor in India, but he became ill and had to give
up his practice and return to England. Here he met my
mother—who was a widow—and they married. My
mother died a few years ago, and my twin sister and I
continued to live with Dr. Roylott until my sister died two
years ago. That is why I am so frightened now!"

"I think you had better tell me all about your sister's
death," Holmes said thoughtfully, drawing on his pipe.

"We live a very odd life, Mr. Holmes. My stepfather's
illness left him a little strange. He has a terrible temper, and
we have no friends or visitors. It is even hard to keep

servants. But my sister met a man in the village and became engaged to marry him. Two weeks before the wedding, she came to me and asked if I had heard a strange whistling sound the night before. I told her I hadn't and she went off to bed."

Miss Stoner shivered, and Holmes threw another log on the fire and drew her chair nearer.

"Something woke me in the night," she continued. "I don't know what it was, but I felt that my sister was in danger. I went to her room. Her door was locked, and I heard a low whistle and a sound of metal clanking. Suddenly the key turned in the lock. Slowly the door opened. My sister stood there in the doorway. Her eyes were terrified. She fell into my arms and cried: 'Helen! It was the speckled band. The speckled band!' And she died."

"What was the cause of her death?" I asked.

"That is what is so frightening, Dr. Watson," she answered. "The police could never discover what killed her. There was no sign of violence or poison. Her door had been locked from the inside and her window had been closed and barred."

"In other words," Holmes said, "she was entirely alone in the room when she was killed."

"That is right, Mr. Holmes."

"What brings you here to me now?" he asked.

"Mr. Holmes, I am to be married in a month. Some repairs are going to be made to my own room. Yesterday Dr. Roylott asked me to sleep in my sister's room. Last night I was awakened by the sound of the same low whistle I heard two years ago! I am terrified that what happened to my sister will happen to me!"

"I think the best thing for me to do, Miss Stoner," Holmes said, "is to visit your home in Surrey. Could we come this afternoon without your stepfather knowing about it?"

"Yes. He has business in the village all afternoon."

"Very good. Return home now, and we will see you later."

A few minutes later we were startled by the crash of the door flying open, and saw a huge man standing in the opening.

"Which of you is Holmes?" he thundered.

"My name, sir," said my companion quietly.

"I am Dr. Grimesby Roylott. I have traced my stepdaughter here. What has she been saying to you?"

"It is a little cold for the time of the year," said Holmes.

"What has she been saying to you?" screamed the old man.

"But I have heard the crocuses promise well," continued my companion calmly.

"Ha! I have heard of you, you scoundrel. You are Holmes, the meddler—Holmes, the busybody!"

Holmes chuckled. "When you go out, please close the door," said he.

"I will go when I have had my say. Don't meddle with my affairs. I am a dangerous man to tangle with! See here." He stepped forward, took the iron poker, and bent it into a curve with his huge brown hands.

"See that you keep yourself out of my grip." He strode out of the room.

"He seems a very friendly person," said Holmes, laughing. He then left on some errands, and returned a few hours later.

"I am on to something, Watson!" he exclaimed. "Look at this copy of the will left by Miss Stoner's mother. Mrs. Roylott left her husband and each of her daughters a one-third share of a thousand pounds a year income. Dr. Roylott has control of the money until the girls marry. At that time, they receive their share. With the one sister dead, Dr. Roylott and Miss Stoner each share half the thousand pounds for the upkeep of the house. This means that if Helen Stoner marries, Dr. Roylott would lose an income of five hundred pounds a year!"

16

"Do you mean to say, Holmes, that you think Roylott killed his first stepdaughter and now means to kill Miss Stoner?"

Holmes did not pause to reply. "Come on, Watson. We must hurry! I believe Helen Stoner's life is in grave danger!"

Miss Stoner was waiting for us in the gloomy old house in Surrey. We followed her as she led us through the house.

"I would like to see your sister's room first," Holmes said.

"All three bedrooms are in this one wing," she replied. "My room is there on the end, and my sister's room is here in the middle. Dr. Roylott has the room next door."

The room where her sister had been killed was square with one door opening into the hall and a single window.

"Is the furniture in the same place as when your sister was alive?" Holmes asked.

"Yes. The bed is clamped to the floor so that it cannot be moved."

"And this rope hanging by the bed? Is that to ring for the maid?" he continued.

"Yes, but it does not work."

Holmes examined it thoughtfully. "It seems to be attached through that hole in the wall."

I looked to where he was pointing and saw a long, narrow ventilator cut through the wall.

"Your stepfather's room is on the other side of this wall, isn't it?" Holmes asked, standing on a chair to measure the hole.

"Yes. I can show you that room if you would like."

We followed her next door. Dr. Roylott's room contained a single bed, a dresser, a table and chair, and a large steel safe.

"My stepfather keeps his business papers in the safe," she explained.

"Does he also keep a cat in here?" Holmes asked.

"Why, no. We have no cat. Why do you ask?"

18

"There on the floor is a small dish of milk." For several moments he stared thoughtfully out the window. "Miss Stoner," he said at last, "would it be possible for you to sleep in your own room without Dr. Roylott knowing?"

"Yes. The workmen have not started there yet."

"Good! You must stay there tonight. Do not leave your room for any reason. Your life depends upon it! Watson and I will spend the night in your sister's room."

It was a night of terrible waiting. I sat in a chair with a pistol in my lap. Holmes sat on the edge of the bed holding a wooden cane. He would not allow us to speak or even light a candle.

The clock had just struck three when I heard a gentle sound like steam escaping from a kettle. In a flash, Holmes struck a match and began beating furiously at the bell-rope by the bed. I could see nothing, but suddenly a horrible cry broke the silence.

"Come quickly, Watson," he called as he ran out and opened the door to Dr. Roylott's room. There in the chair sat the doctor. His eyes were wide and staring—with the look of death. Around his head was a strange yellow band with brown speckles.

"The band! The speckled band!" Holmes exlaimed.

Suddenly the strange band began to move, and from the back of Roylott's head appeared the diamond-shaped head and thick neck of a snake.

"Stay where you are, Watson. It is an adder—the deadliest snake in India!"

Carefully he took a long, thin piece of rope from his pocket and looped it around the snake's neck. With a jerk he caught the snake, threw it into the open safe, and slammed the door shut.

"You knew about the snake, Holmes?" I asked.

"I was fairly certain when I saw the ventilator hole. A real air vent would be built into an outside wall. The bell-rope was also a dummy. Dr. Roylott fixed the bed so that it could not be moved away from the rope. The snake could then

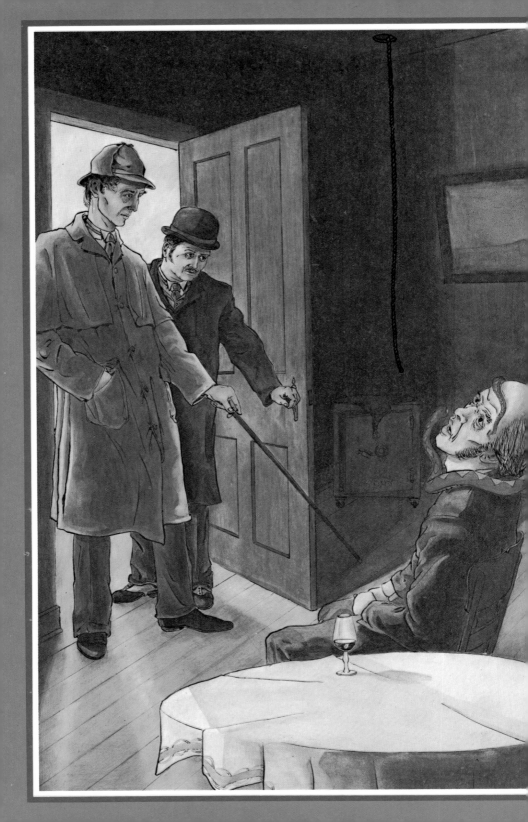

crawl through the hole and down the rope to the bed. He used the milk to train the snake so that when he whistled it would crawl back up the rope and through the hole. The metal clanking Miss Stoner heard was the sound of the safe closing after the snake had returned."

"An evil plan, Holmes. But how could he be sure that the snake would strike his victim?"

"He couldn't. He sent it down night after night knowing that sooner or later his plot would succeed—which it did with Miss Stoner's sister."

"So it looked to the police as though she was alone in the room when she was killed."

"They did not think to look for the very small holes made by the snake's fangs, Watson."

"But what happened tonight?" I asked.

"When I heard the sound of the snake hissing, I struck the bell-rope. The snake became frightened and returned through the hole, biting the first person it saw—Dr. Roylott. I was sure that it would do just that. You might say that I was responsible for his death. Do you know, my dear Watson, I can't even say I am sorry! Shall we go tell Miss Stoner that she is safe now?"

SILVER BLAZE

3

Sherlock Holmes put the newspaper on the table and looked at me thoughtfully. "I am afraid, Watson, that we are going to have to go to Dartmoor," he said.

I did not need to ask why. Only one case now filled the newspapers that could capture the interest of my brilliant friend. All England was talking about Silver Blaze. Three days before, the famous race horse disappeared from his stable in Dartmoor, and his trainer John Straker was found murdered. The race for the Wessex Cup was only a few days off, and Silver Blaze had been picked as the favorite to win.

"There is still no trace of the horse?" I asked.

"None. But the police have arrested a man—Fitzroy Simpson—for the murder of Straker." Holmes rose from the table. "I want to check on some facts, Watson. Meet me at the station in an hour."

Later, when Holmes and I were comfortably settled on the train, my friend explained the details of the case.

"It is a strange case, Watson," he began. "Silver Blaze was very carefully guarded. The door of the stables was kept locked, and Straker had the only key. Dogs guarded the entrance, and three stableboys stayed with Silver Blaze night and day. While one stood watch, the other two slept in the hayloft overhead. On the night Silver Blaze disappeared, Straker's maid was on her way to the stables with the guard's dinner. She found Fitzroy Simpson snooping around outside. She ordered him to leave, and then handed the dinner to the stableboy through a window. The guard saw Simpson and called the dogs to scare him away. But before Simpson ran off, the maid claims she saw him lean in the window."

"Whatever for?" I asked.

"The police believe that he put opium in the guard's food."

"You had best explain, Holmes!" I exclaimed.

"I am trying, my dear fellow! The maid went back to the house and told Straker that Simpson was outside. The trainer went out to look around. He never came back. Mrs. Straker and the maid went out looking for him. They found his body some distance from the stables. A knife was in his hand, but he had been killed by a terrible blow to his head."

"Did the police find the murder weapon?"

"No, Watson. All they found near the body were matches and some burned-out candles stuck in the ground."

"What about Silver Blaze?" I asked.

"When Mrs. Straker went back to the stables for help, she found the door wide open. The two stableboys were still asleep in the loft, the dogs were inside, and the guard on duty had been drugged. Silver Blaze was missing."

"And the police believe that this Fitzroy Simpson stole the horse and killed Straker when the trainer caught him?" I said.

"That's right, Watson," Holmes answered thoughtfully. "But if Simpson did put the drug into the boy's food, it does not explain how he was able to get into the locked stable. And if Simpson did kill Straker, what happened to the horse?"

"Why would anyone want to steal Silver Blaze anyway?" I asked.

"To keep him out of the race, Watson. The Mapleton Stables, for instance, have a horse running in the Wessex Cup race. With Silver Blaze out of the way, their horse is favored to win."

"But surely the police searched the Mapleton Stables for the missing horse, Holmes!" I exclaimed.

"Of course, Watson, but they could find nothing."

"And what do you hope to find at Dartmoor, Holmes?"

"We will just have to see, my friend," Holmes replied and leaned back in his seat to stare thoughtfully out the window.

Inspector Gregory met us at Dartmoor. "Delighted to see you, Holmes!" he said. "Let me introduce you to Colonel Ross. He is the owner of Silver Blaze."

"Good day, Ross," Holmes said. "Inspector, would you be good enough to point out the stables and show me where Straker's body was found?"

"Of course. Mrs. Straker found her husband just over that hill, down in a ravine," the inspector replied.

"May I see the knife you found in his hand, Inspector?"

"Right here, Holmes." The inspector unwrapped a thin, sharp knife.

"What do you make of it, Watson?" Holmes asked as he handed me the knife.

I looked at it carefully. "It is the kind of knife we doctors use in operating," I said. "It is very sharp and delicate."

"That is what I thought!" Holmes exclaimed. "Come, Watson, and we will take a look around."

We left the inspector and Colonel Ross and set off across the moors. We passed some woods and a few sheep, who all seemed to be lame. I could see nothing of interest.

"What are we looking for, Holmes?" I asked.

"Just keep walking, Watson. We are headed in the direction of the Mapleton Stables, a couple of miles away."

We had not gone much farther when Holmes stopped and examined the ground. "Do you see, Watson," he said. "There are prints from a horse's shoes here in the soft dirt."

Quickly we followed the trail of prints. Several times we lost them on rocky ground, but each time we picked them up again farther on.

"Holmes! Look! Here you can see that the horse is not alone. There are footprints of a man walking beside him!" I exclaimed.

"Yes," Holmes replied, "and if you had noticed earlier, you would have seen that we have come in a circle. Now the trail leads directly over there to the Mapleton Stables!"

"Hey!" said a sharp voice behind us. "What do you two want? We don't allow no strangers around here!"

"Mr. Silas Brown?" Holmes asked smoothly as he turned to face the man. "You are the trainer for Mapleton Stables, I believe. We have just come by to see how Silver Blaze is getting along."

"I don't know what you're talking about!" Silas Brown blustered.

"Oh, I think you do!" Holmes said. "Three days ago you found Silver Blaze wandering alone on the moors. At first you were going to return him to Colonel Ross, but you changed your mind. With Silver Blaze out of the way, you had a good chance of winning the Wessex Cup. You circled around and brought him back here. In fact he is over there in that stall. All I need to do is wash off the black dye you used to cover up his white markings."

"How did you know?" Brown cried.

"Oh, you were clever, Brown, but not clever enough."

"Are you going to call the police?" the trainer asked.

"No. Not if you will see that Silver Blaze is returned to his rightful owner as soon as possible. There is still plenty of time to get him ready for the Wessex Cup race."

A short time later we were back at the Dartmoor Stables with Inspector Gregory, Silver Blaze, and a grateful Colonel Ross.

"But if Silver Blaze was not stolen," the inspector said, "what did happen? And who killed John Straker?"

"The killer is standing right here with us," Holmes said smiling.

"Are you suggesting that I killed my trainer?" Ross exclaimed.

"Certainly not!" Holmes ran his hand over the horse's shiny black coat. "This is our killer!"

The two men stood thunderstruck. "Silver Blaze killed

Straker? I think you had better explain, Holmes," the inspector said.

"Straker was heavily in debt," Holmes said. "I also found that he had bet heavily against Silver Blaze winning the race. But let me explain what happened the night he was killed:

"Before the maid took the stableboy his food, Straker slipped opium into the meal. Simpson had nothing to do with any of this, but he did give Straker an excuse to leave the house. Once the boy was asleep, Straker unlocked the stable and took Silver Blaze out over the hill."

"But why?" I asked.

"So no one could watch his evil work. You should know, Watson, that an animal can easily be made slightly lame by making a small cut in the tendons on the back of the leg. It would hardly be noticed, but it would keep a horse from winning a race. That was Straker's plan. Silver Blaze, however, must have sensed some kind of danger. When Straker moved behind him to make the cut in the leg, the horse kicked out and struck the trainer in the head—killing him instantly. The horse then ran away, and he was later found by Silas Brown."

"How did you know, Holmes?" the inspector asked.

"Whoever took Silver Blaze out of the stables," Holmes said, "had to be someone the dogs and horse knew well. Otherwise the animals would have made enough noise to wake up the stableboys in the hayloft. That could have only been Straker, who also had the only key. Then there was the unusual knife he had in his hand. It was too delicate to be a weapon. Also, you will notice that the stray sheep around here are lame. Straker had practiced on them. Finally, there were the candles he had put in the ground for light. Very simple, you see, when you stop to examine the facts."

"You've won again, Holmes!" I said with great pride.

"No, my friend," Holmes smiled. "We will hope Silver Blaze does that for us!"

THE MAN WITH THE TWISTED LIP

4

The gloomy opium den was filled with heavy brown smoke. Carefully I walked down the row of cots. Some of the men were sleeping, while others watched me with dull, dark eyes as they smoked their pipes. I turned as I felt a tug on my coat. At my side was an old man, wrinkled and bent, an opium pipe hanging from his lips.

"Wait for me outside, Watson," he said softly in a voice I recognized very well.

I hurried out into the clean air and I didn't have long to wait before I heard the shuffling steps of the old man behind me.

"Holmes?" I asked cautiously.

"Quiet, Watson. I'll explain why I sent for you once we are well away from this den of evil."

Sherlock Holmes and I must have walked for five minutes before he removed his wig and straightened his body. In an instant, the old man disappeared before my eyes and Holmes was himself again.

"What is all this?" I asked.

"I am working on a case, Watson. Come with me now, and I will explain it to you. I think you will find it interesting."

He turned down a narrow street away from the waterfront, and there his carriage was waiting.

"We are going to see my client—a Mrs. Neville St. Clair. I am trying to find her husband, and he was last seen in that house we just left."

"He was addicted to opium?" I asked.

"No. The opium den is only on the ground floor. The rooms above are rented out. But many people have been known to enter that house and never leave it alive."

"How does Mrs. St. Clair know that her husband was there?"

"It is all very strange," Holmes replied thoughtfully. "Three days ago St. Clair left for work as usual. They have a country home outside the city, but he works in London. That afternoon Mrs. St. Clair received a telegram from a shipping company down here on the docks. A package she had been waiting for had arrived. She came into the city and picked up her package. On her way back up the street, she happened to look up at a window on the second floor of that opium den. Through the window she could see her husband. He gave a cry and threw up his hands, and then he disapeared from sight."

"Goodness, Holmes! What a shock for the poor woman!"

"Yes, Watson. She ran inside and went toward the stairs leading to the second floor, but the manager of the opium den refused to let her past. So she went back out into the street. As luck would have it, a policeman was just passing by. She explained what had happened, and he went back into the house with her. He demanded to see the upstairs room."

"Had Mr. St. Clair rented that room?"

"No, Watson. The room was rented to a beggar named Hugh Boone. He was there when Mrs. St. Clair and the policeman arrived, but there was no sign of Neville St. Clair. The policeman searched the room and found St. Clair's clothes hidden behind the curtains of the back window. His coat, however, was missing, and on the window sill were splotches of blood."

"Was there any sign of St. Clair's body out in back?" I asked.

"The house is built out over the river, Watson."

"So you think this man Boone killed St. Clair and threw his body into the river?"

"That seems to be the only explanation," Holmes answered. "The only fact that seems certain is that Boone was the last person to see St. Clair alive!"

"What have you found out about this man Boone?" I inquired.

"He is a professional beggar, Watson. To avoid the law, he sells matches. I have seen him before on the street corner near that house. He is ragged and dirty and has bright red hair. His face is scarred from the corner of his eye down to his mouth. The scar makes one lip twist up on the end in a sneer. But in spite of his looks and dirt, he is very popular in the area. A great many people gather around him. Some come to stare, but others come to talk to him. He always has a quick remark or a witty reply to make to his customers."

"What could a gentleman like St. Clair have to do with a beggar like this man Boone?" I asked puzzled.

"That is what I was trying to discover today, Watson. The police have arrested Boone for St. Clair's murder and are holding him in the Bow Street prison. Yesterday they found St. Clair's coat in the river. The pockets had been filled with rolls of coins to weight it down. Ah, here we are at the St. Clair home."

Mrs. St. Clair met us at the door. She was a pretty blonde woman, and her eyes were bright and eager as she took us into the drawing room.

"Mr. Holmes," she cried. "Take this envelope. It is a letter from my husband!"

Holmes drew out a single sheet of paper. The letter contained only two lines of writing: *My dear, do not worry. It has all been a mistake. Be patient! Neville.*

"Are you sure this is your husband's writing?" Holmes asked.

"Oh, yes, Mr. Holmes. I am very sure. I can tell that he wrote it in a great hurry, and the paper is old and dirty. Still, I know it is from him."

"What do you make of it, Holmes?" I asked.

33

"I don't know, Watson. I just don't know," he answered.

Holmes was very quiet on the drive back to Baker Street. That night while I slept, he sat in his chair smoking thoughtfully on his pipe. The next morning, he awoke me before the sun was up.

"Come on, Watson! I believe I have found the solution to this case. You, my dear friend, are looking at one of the biggest fools in London!"

Together we went to Bow Street. "I would like to see Hugh Boone, Inspector," Holmes said.

We were taken to a cell down the hall where Boone still lay sleeping on his cot. Once inside, Holmes worked very quietly. He opened a bag he carried and took out a large sponge. He wet it in a pail of water and moved over to the sleeping man. Before Boone could know what was happening, Holmes ran the sponge firmly down the side of the beggar's dirty face. To my amazement, both the dirt and the scar washed away. As Boone sat up, Holmes snatched off the red wig the man wore.

"Why, it is Neville St. Clair!" the Inspector cried. "I recognize him from the picture his wife gave us!"

St. Clair—or Boone—put his head in his hands and moaned.

"I think you had better tell us all about it, man," Holmes said kindly. "After all, you have committed no crime. You can hardly stand trial for murdering yourself!"

"But I don't want my wife and children to find out!"

"I see no reason why they should, unless you tell them. If you tell the police the whole story, I think you can trust the Inspector to keep it out of the newspapers."

St. Clair shuddered, but he had a look of hope on his face. "As a young man," he began, "I worked as an actor. Then I took a job as a newspaper reporter here in London. One day the editor asked me to do an article on the beggars in London. To get the story, I posed as a beggar. While I worked as an actor, I learned to be very good at stage make-up. So I put on a wig, dirtied my face, and made a fake scar down one cheek. With a piece of tape I fixed my lip on one side to give it an odd twist. I took some matches to sell and found a good corner for my begging.

"Mr. Holmes, I made more in one day of begging than I did in a whole week working at the newspaper! I am not saying that every beggar makes as much, but I have a gift for talking to people. They come to me not only to buy matches, but to exchange witty remarks. They always give me extra money.

"So, I gave up my job as a reporter and began begging full time. I made a very good income, and soon could afford to marry and buy a home in the country. My wife thinks I work at some job in the city.

"Then last Monday, I was in the room I rent as Hugh Boone. There I changed from my disguise as a beggar to my business suit. I was standing at the window when my wife looked up and saw me. I knew the manager of the opium den downstairs would try to stop her from coming up. That gave me just enough time to get back into my rags, put on my make-up, and hide my clothes behind the curtains. I had put the money I made that day into the pocket of my coat. I threw it out the window, hoping to get it later. But I was in such a hurry that I cut my finger on a piece of metal on the window sill. That is why the police found blood."

"And so when the police arrived," Holmes said, "you preferred to be arrested for the murder of Neville St. Clair rather than have your wife know the truth!"

"Yes!" he cried. "Can you really keep my past a secret, Inspector?"

"I can," the Inspector replied. "But Hugh Boone has got to disappear! There can be no more of this double life!"

"I swear, Inspector, after what I have been through these last three days, I will never do it again!"

"I wish I knew how you figured it out, Holmes," I said as we returned to Baker Street.

"All it took, my dear Watson," Holmes replied, "was a sleepless night and six pipes of tobacco!"

THE RED-HEADED LEAGUE

5

I called in Baker Street one day to see my friend Sherlock Holmes, and found him with a new client. "Come in, Watson. Come in," he said. "I want you to meet Mr. Jabez Wilson. He has a most unusual story."

Jabez Wilson gave me a nod of greeting, and I studied him with interest. He was obviously from the working class. His clothes fit loosely, and he had a full head of flaming red hair.

Holmes noticed my interest. He shook his head with a smile. "Beyond the obvious facts that he has at some time done manual labor, that he has been in China, and that he has done a great deal of writing lately, I can tell nothing else."

Mr. Jabez Wilson sat up in his chair. "How did you know all that, Mr. Holmes? It's true that I did manual labor, for I began as a ship's carpenter."

"Your hands, dear sir. Your right hand is larger and more muscular than the left."

"And the writing?"

"What else can be shown by that shiny right sleeve, and the left one with the smooth patch near the elbow where you rest it on the desk?"

"Well, but China?"

"The fish that is tattooed above your wrist could only have been done in China. I have made a small study of tattoo marks."

Mr. Wilson laughed. "At first I thought you were clever, but I see there is nothing in it, after all."

"I begin to think, Watson," said Holmes, "that I made a mistake in explaining. Mr. Wilson, please begin your story again for Dr. Watson."

"Well," Wilson began, "I ran a small pawnshop over in Coburg Square. One day my assistant—Vincent Spaulding—brought in this advertisement from the newspaper."

He reached in his pocket and drew out a small clipping that read: "One membership now open in Red-headed League. Four pounds weekly will be paid for simple office work. Apply in person to Duncan Ross." And a date, time, and address in Fleet Street followed.

"Strange, isn't it, Watson?" Holmes laughed. "But continue, Wilson. What is this Red-headed League?"

"I had never heard of it either, Mr. Holmes," Wilson said. "But Vincent had. A wealthy man with red hair set up a fund to help other red-headed men. To join the League, a man had to have bright red hair—like mine—and be in need of extra money."

He paused and pulled out a handkerchief to mop his red face.

"Mr. Holmes, I had never seen anything like it! When Vincent and I got to the building in Fleet Street, there was a huge crowd of red-headed men waiting. One after another the men in front of me were turned away. Then my turn came. Right away Duncan Ross seemed to like me. He asked a few questions and then offered me a place in the League and the job."

"What were you expected to do for your four pounds a week?" Holmes asked.

"I was to work for four hours a day from Monday to Friday right there in that room. My job was to copy the encyclopedia—beginning with the letter A. The only rule was that I could not leave the office for any reason. If I did, I would lose the job and my place in the League. For eight weeks I have been going to the office to do my work, Mr. Holmes. At first Ross stayed with me for at least part of the day to make sure I didn't leave. Finally, he only came in at the end of the week to pay me. Then this morning I went to the office as usual. I am just about finished with the A's. I have copied out everything from Aardvark to Aztec. When I arrived, I found this note tacked to the door and the office locked."

He handed Holmes a card with the following message:

THE RED-HEADED LEAGUE IS DISSOLVED.
OCTOBER 9, 1890.

"I talked to the landlord," Wilson continued. "He had never heard of Duncan Ross. The room had been rented by a man named Morris. But when I went to Mr. Morris' address, I found it was a factory that made wooden legs!"

This was too much for Holmes and I. We both burst out laughing. "I apologize, Wilson," Holmes said. "But you must admit that the whole thing sounds quite absurd!"

"Yes, it does," Wilson admitted. "But why would someone want to play such a joke on me? That's what I want to find out."

"Have you found anything missing from the shop?" I asked.

"No, nothing. Nor has anything been taken from my apartment over the shop."

"Tell me more about your assistant—Vincent Spaulding," Holmes said. "Has he been with you long?"

"He came to work for me about a month before the advertisement came out. He offered to work for half pay if I would teach him the pawnbrokers' trade."

"Half pay!" Holmes exclaimed. "He sounds like an unusual man. Have you found him a good worker?"

"He is an excellent worker except for his hobby. He is always taking pictures with his camera and then dashing

40

down to the cellar to develop them. But he gets the work done."

"What does he look like?" Holmes continued. "Is he young?"

"Not really. He is about thirty, small, very quick in his ways, and he has a small white scar on his forehead."

"Does he by any chance have his ears pierced for earrings?" Holmes asked, very much excited.

"Why, yes. He said the gypsies did it years ago."

"Humm!" Holmes murmured thoughtfully. "Is he still with you?"

"Oh, yes. I have just left him."

"Thank you very much, Mr. Wilson. Let me see. Today is Friday. I will have an answer for you within the next two days."

"Watson," Holmes said when our visitor had gone, "I think this is a much more serious business than I thought at first. But come. We will visit Coburg Square. I believe the answer is there."

When we arrived at the pawnshop, Holmes did not go in. Instead he walked up and down the street and then went through the alley to the street beyond. Coburg Square was a very quiet place, but the next street over was a busy business area. Carefully Holmes looked at the stores, the restaurants, and the Coburg branch of the City Bank. He walked back through the alley deep in thought, his cane thumping heavily on the pavement.

"I must leave you now, Watson," he said at last. "If you would like to see the end of this case, meet me in Baker Street at ten o'clock tonight."

Promptly at ten I arrived at Holmes' house. With him were a police inspector from Scotland Yard and a man I did not know.

"Watson, let me introduce you to Mr. Merryweather. He is president of the City Bank."

Now, I don't consider myself to be any stupider than the

next man, but I couldn't see for the life of me what Holmes was up to. He led us to Mr. Merryweather's carriage, and we went off to the Coburg branch of the City Bank. Once inside, the four of us climbed down the stone steps to the basement of the building.

"Do you see those crates, Watson?" Holmes asked, pointing to several wooden crates that lined the walls. "They hold 30,000 pounds in gold. They are to be shipped Monday to the Bank of France. Now, if you will close the lid on the lantern, we will wait. I warn you all, you must not make a single sound."

For nearly an hour we sat silent in the dark. Then a light appeared through a crack in the stone floor. The crack grew bigger and bigger, and the head and shoulders of a man came through the hole.

"Quickly, Watson!" Holmes called. "Open the lantern!"

At the same moment, he grabbed the man in the center of the room. "It is no use, John Clay," he said calmly. "The police are waiting for your friends inside the pawnshop."

"What is all this, Holmes?" I asked.

"This man is John Clay—or Vincent Spaulding as he has been calling himself lately. The police have been trying to catch him for some time now. You can arrest him, Inspector, for attempted burglary!"

"But how did you know what John Clay planned for tonight, Holmes?" I asked when we were back in Baker Street.

He leaned back in his chair and drew contentedly on his pipe. "The facts were all there, Watson. It was really very simple. The only reason for something as silly as the Red-headed League was to get the pawnbroker out of his shop for several hours every day. But why? Nothing was taken from the shop, so his assistant had to have some other reason. The first clue was that Clay—or Spaulding—was always going down to the cellar. Then, when Mr. Wilson described Vincent Spaulding, I recognized him as John

Clay—a very dangerous criminal. I have a note on him in my files.

"The matter became obvious when I saw that the City Bank lay directly behind the pawnshop. And when I pounded the pavement with my cane, I found that it was hollow underneath. That could only mean that Clay and his friend Duncan Ross had used those weeks alone in the shop to dig a tunnel from the pawnshop to the basement of the Bank. You will also remember that Vincent Spaulding had agreed to work for half pay—a most unusual man."

"But how did you know that they would try to steal the gold tonight?"

"Think, my dear Watson! The tunnel must have been finished or they would not have dissolved the League. The gold was to be moved on Monday. By taking it tonight, they would have two days to get away before the robbery was discovered. Simple, my dear friend!"

"Holmes," I said sincerely, "you never cease to amaze me! You are a true servant of mankind!"

"It keeps me from being bored, Watson." Holmes yawned and lit another pipe. "Yes, it keeps me from being bored."

GLOSSARY

arrest (ə rest′) to take someone under control by authority of the law

blackmail (blak′ māl′) to force someone to pay money by threatening to reveal a secret about that person

criminal (krim′ ən əl) a person who has broken the law

disappear (dis′ ə piər′) to stop being visible, or become lost from sight

disguise (dis gīz′) to change clothing and looks so as to hide identity

murder (mərd′ ər) to purposefully kill a human being

opium (ō′ pē əm) an addictive drug that is the dried juice of a kind of poppy

pawnshop (pȯn′ shäp′) a place where a person leaves something of value in exchange for money borrowed

recognize (rek′ əg nīz′) to know a person upon sight

scandal (skan′ dəl) talk or disturbance that hurts a person's standing and reputation